To
Cory

Follow your Heart
to chase the Rainbows of
Life

Take care
R Dau Dee
1996

The Legend of
SPINOZA™
The Bear Who Speaks from the Heart

ROBERT TALLTREE

illustrated by Stéphanie Roth

A SPINOZA™ BOOK
from
UNIVERSAL
TRADEWINDS PUBLISHING

SAINT PAUL, MINNESOTA

Author's Note & Acknowledgements

Ojibwe:

Makwa – Bear

miigwech – thank you

L/Dakota:

mitakuye oyasin – to all my relatives (we are all related)

Chantay (Ćante) – Heart

As an Ojibwe I have made many friends of both nations, and so it is with the greatest respect for my brothers and sisters of the L/Dakota and Ojibwe nations that I use these words in this story to recognize and appreciate the unique differences of each tribe, and also to recognize the similarities, for it is the sacred hoop of life that brings us all together as one people.

I would like to thank everyone at Universal Tradewinds for their commitment to this book, Sheri Sundby for her friendship and love for Spinoza the Bear, Jane Noland, whose talent in the art of expression helped me to bring forth my own writing, and Nancy Tuminelly for her personal touch and insight in this project.

— Robert TallTree

Copyright © 1995 by Universal Tradewinds Inc.

All Rights Reserved. No part of this book may be reproduced in any form, except for brief reviews, without written permission of the publisher. For information about permission, write to: Permissions, Universal Tradewinds Publishing, 245 East 6th Street, Saint Paul, MN 55101-1940.

Library of Congress Cataloging-in-Publication Data

94-61833

ISBN 0-9643529-0-7

Conceptualized by Terri Lynn
Edited by Jane Noland
Design and production by MacLean & Tuminelly
The color illustrations are done in Grumbacher watercolors and Prisma color pencil on Arches 90 pound Cold Press watercolor paper. The display type is set in Prague and Poetica, and the text type is set in Caslon Antique, composed by MacLean & Tuminelly.

H 10 9 8 7 6 5 4 3 2 1

Color separations by Encore Color Group, Eagan, Minnesota.
Printing and binding by Worzalla Printing, Stevens Point, Wisconsin.
Paper supplied by Turnquist, Inc.

Universal Tradewinds Publishing
245 East 6th Street
Saint Paul, MN 55101-1940
U.S.A.
(612) 227-3717

Printed in U.S.A.

Dedication

I wish to say miigwech to the Creator, from whom all great things begin.
And Terri Lynn, whose compassion and love for humanity inspired this story.

For my children – Brandi, Cinamyn, and Robert, and my granddaughter, Ashley Kay.

And for Spinoza, because the greatest gift of all is love.

Mitakuye Oyasin
Robert TallTree

M any years ago
in a land deep in the heart of the great north woods
there was a valley where an ancient tribe lived
in harmony with all of nature.
They called themselves "The People."

Their small Indian village was nestled
at the end of a valley
where a waterfall cascaded down
past an abundance of red cedar trees.

The roots of the trees extended gracefully into the water,
which tasted sweet,
and The People were happy
to make this place
their home.

They elected a leader
whose honesty and courage
earned The People's trust,
and he was able to make peace
among all the tribes.

Because of his great wisdom,
    many came to seek his counsel.
        He held the name of Makwa,
            which, in the language of The People,
                means Bear.

    Makwa was humble
        and knew that it was good to follow
            the traditional way
                of respecting the teachings of the elders.

        Soon Makwa would learn
            the importance of these lessons.

For Makwa, now in the fullness of his life,
    the only gift that shone brighter than the morning sun
        was the birth of his only child.

This brought him great happiness, but sadness as well.
    The sadness came at the loss of his beloved wife, Running Deer,
        whose life was given during this birth.

Happiness came as he cradled his newborn son.
He recognized the softness of Running Deer
in the child's gentle features,
and was comforted by
his son's innocence and beauty.

Makwa's son grew tall and slender as a willow.
His eyes, like his mother's, were large and dark,
and they reflected the brightness of the sun.

His smile was kind, and crooked as a half-moon.
Because of this, he was known as Crooked Moon.

Makwa loved his son dearly, and so did the people of the village.
They loved Crooked Moon's sparkling eyes and the way he made them laugh.

When Crooked Moon reached the age of seven winters,
Makwa asked him to gather plants for The People's medicine.

The People were very wise in the nature of plants and used them for many remedies.
Crooked Moon knew this.
He felt proud and honored to be chosen for this important task.

First, he went to see the old basket maker, who said,
  "Here Crooked Moon, is a basket that is just right for your small hands."

  Her name was Broken Smile,
    and her lodge was filled with sweet-smelling baskets
      made of birch, sage, and sweetgrass.

But Crooked Moon replied,
  "Don't you know that I must carry
    not only the best basket,
    but the biggest?"

Broken Smile laughed and said,
  "Then the biggest and best it shall be!"

Next, Crooked Moon
    borrowed his father's moccasins,
        tying them with extra leather
            to keep them on his feet.

He did this because he had heard so many times
    that he would someday walk in Makwa's shoes,
        and Crooked Moon knew
            that this must be that day.

The news of his journey spread
    throughout the village,
        and The People encouraged Crooked Moon
            by saying, "You look like a brave warrior."

This excited Crooked Moon, who stood up as tall as he could,
folding his golden arms and puffing out his chest,
on which he had painted a large bird to scare away evil spirits.

He proudly walked down the trail along the river,
carrying his basket in one hand and a large stick in the other.

He often turned and waved his walking stick
high in the air to his people,
until he could no longer see them.

Crooked Moon tried to remember an honor song
    his father had taught him.
        And, as he walked, he sang it to himself,
            sometimes humming
                when he forgot a word or two,
                    but never slowing his pace.

He came to a place on the river bank
    where he set down his basket and stick
        and began to gather plants.
            Some he knew, like horsetail and wintergreen.
                Some he didn't.

                    Some were ordinary wildflowers,
                        but they were beautiful,
                            so he gathered them anyway,
                        just in case
                    The People might need them.

Crooked Moon worked for what seemed like hours,
filling the birch basket until it became so heavy
he could hardly lift it with both his hands.

He headed back towards the village, lugging his basket,
eager to show his father the fruits of his harvest.

But before long he grew very tired and hungry, too.
The basket seemed to grow bigger and heavier with every step.

Crooked Moon decided right then and there to sit down.
THUNK went the basket as it landed sideways,
spilling out the many-colored plants.

Crooked Moon looked at the scattered plants and let out a big sigh.
Resting his chin in his hand, he said out loud,
"I thought this was going to be fun, but it is a lot of work!
This should be done by someone
at least ten – or even a hundred – winters old,
not someone as little as me!"

All this time his father had been
following and watching,
hidden behind the pine trees.
He knew well that this was the way
his people had been taught
from generation to generation.

And for a moment Makwa remembered
how his father had trusted him
with this same task.
Makwa smiled, wondering
what Crooked Moon would do next.

Makwa watched his son stand,
scoop up what plants he could,
and toss them back into the basket.

Then he saw him take the basket in both hands,
pushing and dragging it
until Crooked Moon was quite exhausted.

Makwa saw his son kick the basket
with the huge moccasins that he noticed
belonged to him!
Makwa covered his mouth
to keep from laughing out loud.

Although Crooked Moon tried and tried,
the basket was too much for him.

Then a smile brightened his face. He had an idea!
One by one, he began taking the plants from the basket,
and tucking them into his buckskin britches.

He stuffed and stuffed and then stuffed some more,
until there was no more room.

Once this was done,
Crooked Moon realized
that he couldn't even bend over,
let alone walk comfortably.
Leaves and flowers
were sticking out everywhere.

Crooked Moon said to himself,
See, I have learned to walk
without bending my knees!

But Crooked Moon hadn't
considered the size
of his father's moccasins.
Even though he had tied them securely,
the toes scuffed with each stiff-legged step.
So he decided it would be easier
to travel with a walking stick.

Since Crooked Moon had forgotten his stick at the river bank,
he decided to pull a branch from a tree that was close to him.

He hadn't noticed that the tree had squirrels living in it.

The squirrels, not taking kindly to their home
being rocked back and forth,
began bouncing acorns off Crooked Moon's head.
They even made loud noises
and twitched their tails
in gestures of anger.

Crooked Moon's eyes became wide with fear.
   Maybe the squirrels were evil spirits
      sent to test him!
         He asked himself, What would a great warrior do?

Then, not really knowing this,
   he began jumping and kicking
      and flapping his arms
         and making loud, hooting sounds
            like an owl.
               Surely this would scare away
                  any evil spirits.

After all, he still had the painting of a large bird upon his chest.

All this noise made the squirrels very nervous,
and they soon scurried on their way.
Crooked Moon raised his fist in triumph and shouted,
"Good! That will teach them to come around me.
After all, I am Crooked Moon,
son of Makwa!"

By this time the sun was near the horizon,
painting the forest floor
with yellows and oranges.
Darkness was near.

As the evening grew cooler,
dew formed on the leaves of the plants
that covered the ground.
The moisture caused the toes
of the moccasins to stiffen
and curve up like canoes.

Crooked Moon's eyes became even bigger.
He feared that Makwa would be angry.

Why did I take my father's favorite moccasins?
Crooked Moon thought in desperation.
What will I do?

Then he remembered – The People used certain plants
when they worked with leather.

"I know about one of them," he said out loud. "It has purple berries."
Maybe it would soften the moccasins.
But only the elders were allowed to touch it.

Oh well, just a little couldn't hurt, he thought.
He began to search around the trees and bushes
until he found the plant he was looking for.

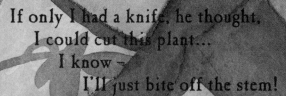

"There it is! Purple berries," he said.
He tried to pick it.
He pulled and pulled,
but the plant was strong
and would not let go of the land.

If only I had a knife, he thought,
I could cut this plant...
I know –
I'll just bite off the stem!

And so he did.

Suddenly he became very sleepy.

Makwa, who was still watching,
knew that the plant could be deadly.
Never before had Makwa felt such fear.

All he could hear
was the sound of his own heart,
beating like thunder to his ears.

He ran to his son, yelling,
"NO! STOP!"

But it was too late.

Makwa cradled Crooked Moon,
who now laid limp in his arms,
and holding his son close to his heart
he ran swiftly back to the village.

The trees and the brush scratched at Makwa's arms and legs,
but he felt nothing.
He knew there was not a moment to lose.

Strong with the hope of saving his son,
Makwa carried Crooked Moon
to the brightly painted lodge
of Chan-tay, the medicine man.

He told the medicine man what had happened.
Chan-tay knew that there was little help
for such a poison,
and with sadness in his eyes
he slowly shook his head.

Then, out of the twilight, they heard a beautiful voice
singing from somewhere deep within the woods.
Chan-tay's eyes brightened.
"There is hope," he said.
He cupped his hand around his ear
and whispered, "Listen."

"What is it?" asked Makwa.

"It is the song of the Spirit Tree," Chan-tay said.
"Follow it.
Listen with your heart,
and you may find the greatest medicine of all."

The sound echoed hauntingly, like whispers in the wind.

Leaving Chan-tay to care for Crooked Moon,
Makwa immediately began his journey through the darkness,
taking an ancient trail
into the deepest part of the woods.

Makwa traveled for many hours,
        guided by the beckoning voice
            and the light of a thin moon.

Thinking only of his great love for his son,
    Makwa would not stop to eat
        or even to quench his thirst at a spring.
    He became weak with hunger and weariness,
and finally he collapsed.

Resting his head on the mossy roots of a tree,
    he was lulled into a deep sleep
        by the mysterious voice
            and the rhythm of the waves
                splashing against the shore
                    of the lake nearby.

Morning came and the dew fell in cool droplets
    from the branches of the tree onto Makwa's brow, waking him.

Am I dreaming? he asked himself.
    He could still hear the beautiful voice, closer now.
        The song stirred feelings deep within his heart
            and drew tears to his eyes
                as he thought of losing his son.

His tears worked their way
    through the lines of wisdom on his face.
        When the tears fell,
            they caressed the roots of a tree.

            Then something magical happened.
                Small sparkles, like stars,
                    rose from the places where his tears had fallen.

And Makwa realized
    that the tree that had sheltered him
        throughout the night
            was the Spirit Tree
                he had been seeking.

                It was a wondrous, towering red cedar,
                    standing alone on a rock cliff at the edge of the forest,
                        its shadow sprawling
                            across the morning calm of the lake.

    Its weathered trunk
        twisted and curved into its limbs,
            reflecting its great age.
                How long it had been there
                    no one could say.

In an ancient language, the Spirit Tree
sang of the meaning of love.
It sang of the birth of each day
and the promise of hope
in the lives of all creatures.

Makwa reached out slowly
to touch the trunk of the tree.
And when he did, the song stopped.
A sturdy branch seemed to float,
light as an eagle feather, into his arms.

He embraced it for a moment,
knowing that this was what he had come for.

Makwa held the branch up to the sky,
and said "Thank you for this gift.
But may I ask for another?
Please help me get back
in time to save my son."

Without a sound,
    a horse appeared beside the Spirit Tree –
a stallion, silent and strong,
and white as new-fallen snow.

It greeted Makwa as if it had known him from birth,
so, without hesitation, he leaped upon its back.
Grasping its mane, he said gently,
    "Take me home."

The stallion's speed was magnificent.
It seemed to ride the wind,
flying through the woods and across the valleys.

It knew the way and carried Makwa to the door
of the medicine man's lodge.

Makwa jumped down from the horse,
and in turning to offer his thanks,
he realized that
the beautiful stallion
had vanished
as quickly as it
had appeared.

Makwa threw back
the deerhide door
and saw that Crooked Moon
still lay motionless.

Holding the branch
in his hand,
he said to Chan-tay,
"How is this to be prepared?
Shall we make a tea?"

Chan-tay said, "This is not a plant for tea.
Listen carefully to your heart and carve a form
that gives shape to these feelings.

The medicine comes
from the tree of hope and love."

With tears in his eyes, Makwa drew his knife
but allowed his heart to work the wood.
So great was Makwa's love
that the piece of wood
began to form
without the touch of the blade.

At first the form almost looked human.
To Makwa's amazement
it was no longer wood –
it had become a bear!

Not a fierce bear,
   but a bear that,
      as it took shape,
became soft and comforting,
      like the warm, winter coats
of the village ponies.

And it seemed to grow larger –
      until it became the size
of a young child.

   As Makwa held the
small, brown bear,
      he remembered a name
that came to him in a dream.
   Although it seemed strange
at the time,
      he realized now
whose name it must be.

"We will call him Spinoza," he said,
      and he laid the bear
in the arms
      of his sleeping son.

In this time,
    as the sun set and rose again,
Spinoza was kept close
    to Crooked Moon's heart.
Makwa stayed by his son,
    hoping for a sound or some slight movement.

        There was none.

Sadly, Makwa turned away.
    Gazing through one of the holes in the doorway,
he looked out at the smoldering fires
    that had burned throughout the night.

As the sun's rays
sent shafts of light through
the small openings of the lodge,
one beam moved across Spinoza,
forming a small heart on his chest.
In the shadows, Makwa thought he saw
Spinoza's eyes sparkle.

Out of the stillness came a small whisper.
"Father, I am thirsty."
It was Crooked Moon.

Makwa's sigh of relief gave way
to a tear that fell gently,
losing itself on the soft, dry sand of the floor.

Spinoza stretched and said, "I'm thirsty,
and I'm hungry too!"

They all began to laugh.
    Makwa embraced his son and the bear, Spinoza,
        and held them both for a long time,
            as if he would never let them go.

Then he threw back the deerhide door of the lodge
    and called out to The People,
        "Crooked Moon is awake,
          and we have a new friend.
            His name is Spinoza!"
             All was well.

But the story doesn't end here...

...because The People accepted Spinoza
as one of the many miracles of life,
and honored him
by asking him to join them
at their council fires,
where Spinoza,
with great love and respect,
would tell them his stories.

As time passed, Spinoza's friendship with Crooked Moon flourished.
They shared their hopes and dreams,
their laughter and their tears –
true companions bonded by love.

Spinoza taught Crooked Moon many things.
Through songs and stories, he often spoke about
the beauty that lies within each of us
and compared us to the flowers –
each of us different, yet needing to share
and respect one another's unique gifts.

He even spoke about how life
is like the passing of the seasons –
how as each season comes,
in its time it must go.

One autumn evening when the moon was full,
as Crooked Moon listened to Spinoza,
he began to understand
how important it is
to believe in yourself
and to follow your dreams.

Spinoza reminded Crooked Moon that love can heal,
and that it doesn't matter how small you are
if your heart is big.

"Yes!" Crooked Moon said,
"That's what makes the difference."

Spinoza nodded and smiled.
"Crooked Moon," he said,
"It's time for me to go."

Crooked Moon felt sad. "Why? Don't you love me?"

Spinoza reached up his arms
   as if to embrace the sky and said,
      "My love for you is beyond any words,
         even beyond the stars."

Then he hugged Crooked Moon and said,
      "My stories are meant to be shared with many people."

Even in his sadness, Crooked Moon knew these words were true.
      He smiled and said,
         "Spinoza, you speak from your heart."

Spinoza gave him a smile,
kind and crooked, like that of a half-moon.
"Here," said Crooked Moon.
"I have something for you,
so you will always remember me."
He reached into the medicine pouch that hung at his waist
and took out a piece of fine, red cloth.

"My father gave this to me, and now I give it to you.
It is a sign that you are very brave."

Crooked Moon tied the cloth around Spinoza's furry neck.
Spinoza hugged him again and said,
"Thank you, Crooked Moon. I will wear this with honor."

Makwa, who stood nearby,
  looked at Crooked Moon with pride,
    realizing how much his son had grown.
      He reached over and placed his hand
        upon Crooked Moon's shoulder.

Together, they waved good-bye
  to the loving little bear.
    Their eyes followed his gentle shape
      as Spinoza turned and headed
        toward the great, bright moon
          that lighted the valley of The People.

Even after he had disappeared
  into the shadows of the woods,
    they could hear him singing,

      "I'm your friend, and my name is Spinoza."

          And so Spinoza's journey begins....

Hi! My name is Spinoza, and I'm a real teddy bear. Just like the legend says, I'm a teller of stories and I sing songs, too! I've taught my songs and stories to thousands of people all over the world, and now I'd like to come to your house to share hugs, stories and songs with you!

To learn more about me, write to: Spinoza (that's me!), 245 East 6th Street, Saint Paul, MN 55101, or call 1-800-CUB-BEAR.

My friends will be happy to tell you more about me, my stories and the places I've been. I'll be out in the Great North Woods, just waiting to hear from you.